Kitten's First Full Moon

KEVIN HENKES
Kitten's
First

Full Moon

 Greenwillow Books
An Imprint of HarperCollinsPublishers

For L, W, C & S

Kitten's First Full Moon. Copyright © 2004 by Kevin Henkes. All rights reserved. Printed in the United States of America. www.harperchildrens.com
Gouache and colored pencil were used to prepare the full-color art. The text type is 22-point Gill Sans Extra Bold.

Library of Congress Cataloging-in-Publication Data. Henkes, Kevin. Kitten's first full moon / by Kevin Henkes.—p. cm.—"Greenwillow Books."
Summary: When Kitten mistakes the full moon for a bowl of milk, she ends up tired, wet, and hungry trying to reach it.
ISBN 0-06-058828-4 (trade). ISBN 0-06-058829-2 (lib. bdg.) [1. Cats—Fiction. 2. Animals—Infancy—Fiction. 3. Moon—Fiction.] I. Title.
PZ7.H389Ki 2004—[E]—dc21 2003012564

First Edition 10 9 8 7 6 5 4 3 2 1

It was Kitten's first full moon.

When she saw it, she thought,

There's a little bowl of milk in the sky.

And she wanted it.

**So she closed her eyes
and stretched her neck
and opened her mouth and licked.**

**But Kitten only ended up
with a bug on her tongue.
Poor Kitten!**

Still, there was the little bowl

of milk, just waiting.

So she pulled herself together
and wiggled her bottom
and sprang from the top step of the porch.

But Kitten only tumbled—
bumping her nose and banging her ear
and pinching her tail.
Poor Kitten!

Still, there was the little bowl

of milk, just waiting.

So she chased it—
down the sidewalk,
   through the garden,
      past the field,
         and by the pond.
But Kitten never seemed to get closer.
Poor Kitten!

Still, there was the little bowl

of milk, just waiting.

So she ran
to the tallest tree
she could find,
and she climbed
and climbed
and climbed
to the very top.

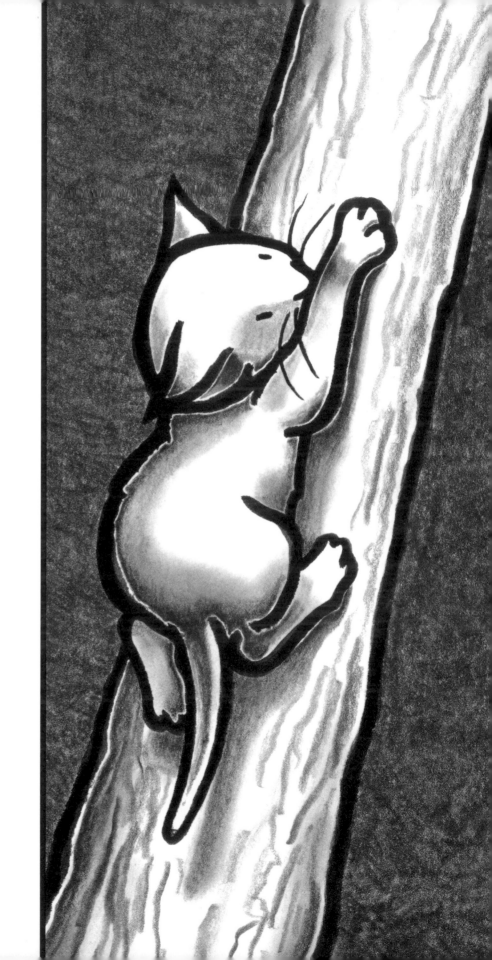

**But Kitten
still couldn't reach
the bowl of milk,
and now she was
scared.
Poor Kitten!
What could she do?**

Then, in the pond, Kitten saw
another bowl of milk.
And it was bigger.
What a night!

**So she raced down the tree
and raced through the grass**

and raced to the edge of the pond.

She leaped with all her might—

Poor Kitten!

She was wet and sad and tired and hungry.

So she went

back home—

and there was

    a great big

bowl of milk

    on the porch,

just waiting for her.

Lucky Kitten!

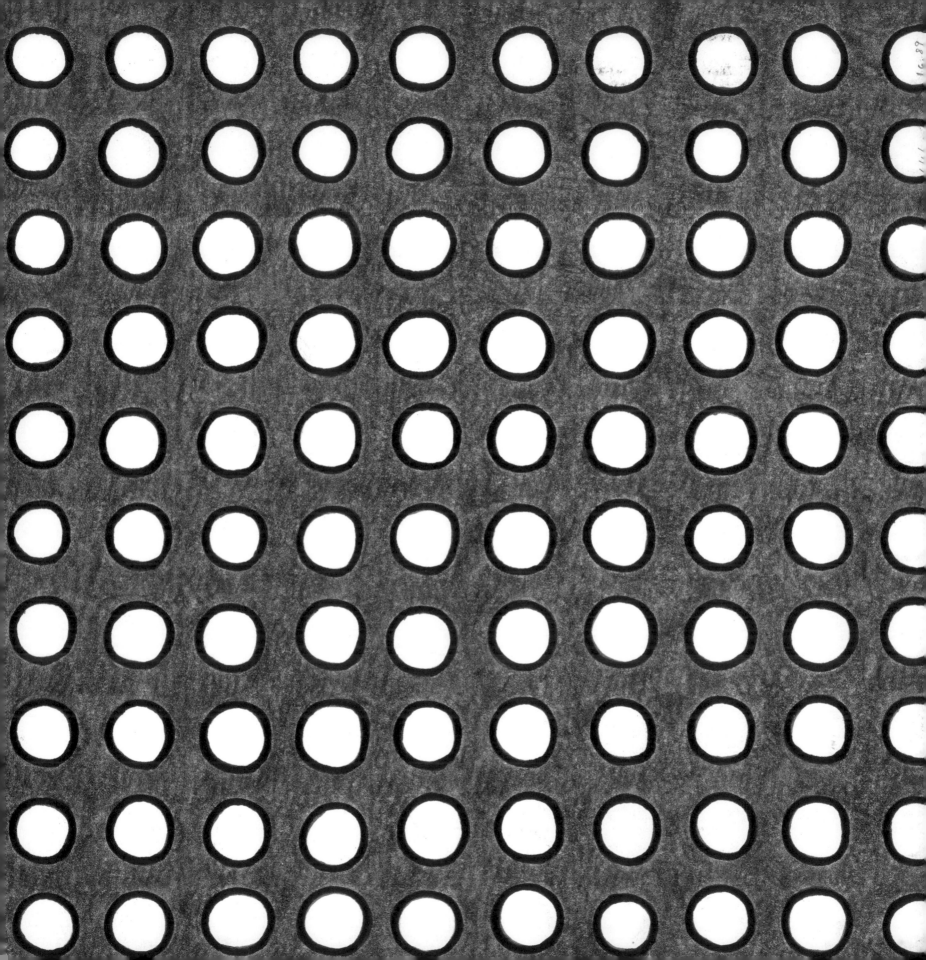